Inside My World

WHERE I LIVE

By Tina Benjamin

Gareth Stevens
PUBLISHING

Please visit our website, www.garethstevens.com. For a free color catalog of all our high-quality books, call toll free 1-800-542-2595 or fax 1-877-542-2596.

Library of Congress Cataloging-in-Publication Data

Benjamin, Tina.
Where I live / by Tina Benjamin.
p. cm. — (Inside my world)
Includes index.
ISBN 978-1-4824-1814-9 (pbk.)
ISBN 978-1-4824-1812-5 (6-pack)
ISBN 978-1-4824-1813-2 (library binding)
1. Cities and towns — Juvenile literature. 2. City and town life — Juvenile literature. I. Benjamin, Tina. II. Title.
HT152.B45 2015
307.76—d23

First Edition

Published in 2015 by
Gareth Stevens Publishing
111 East 14th Street, Suite 349
New York, NY 10003

Editor: Ryan Nagelhout
Designer: Sarah Liddell

Photo credits: Cover, p. 1 Michael Shake/Shutterstock.com; p. 5 spirit of america/Shutterstock.com; pp. 7, 9 Max Topchii/Shutterstock.com; p. 11 Kenneth Sponsler/Shutterstock.com; p. 13 Josef Hanus/Shutterstock.com; p. 15 Scott David Patterson/Shutterstock.com; p. 17 Zurijeta/Shutterstock.com; pp. 19, 24 (fire station) planet5D LLC/Shutterstock.com; pp. 21, 24 (fountain) s_oleg/Shutterstock.com; p. 23 caamalf/Shutterstock.com; p. 24 (pool) Volodymyr Burdiak/Shutterstock.com.

Printed in the United States of America

CPSIA compliance information: Batch #CW15GS: For further information contact Gareth Stevens, New York, New York at 1-800-542-2595.

Contents

I live in a town.

This is my house.
I live here
with my family.

We have a pool!
I love to swim.

I go shopping
with my mom.
We shop
on Main Street.

Gallery
OPEN
GALLERY, INC.

This is my school.
I learn here!

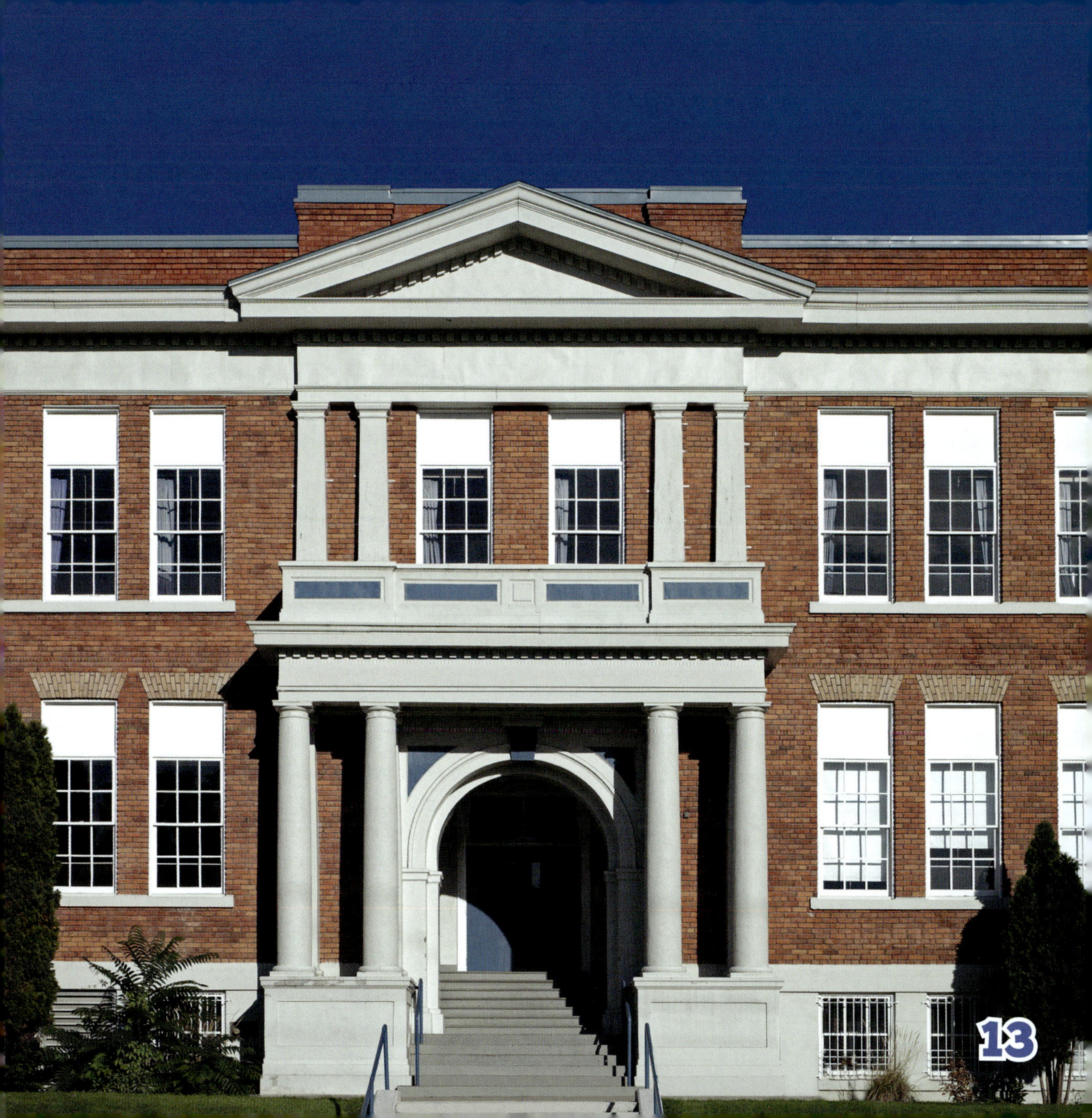

I like to play baseball
in this park.

My friend Henry lives down the street. I walk to his house.

I walk
by the fire station.
Firefighters work there!

FIRE DEPARTMENT

My dad takes me to our town square. There is a fountain in it.

I throw a coin
in the fountain.

Words to Know

fire station

fountain

pool

Index